The ArtScroll Children's Holiday Series

④

Yaffa Ganz

CHANUKAH

WITH BINA, BENNY AND CHAGGAI HAYONAH

Illustrated by Liat Benyaminy Ariel

halom! I'm Chaggai HaYonah — Chaggai the Holiday Dove. Tonight is a special night. It's the twenty-fifth night of the month of Kislev — the first night of Chanukah. Bina and Benny's father has just finished lighting the first candle in the menorah.

"I wish I could have lived in the time of the Chashmonaim," said Benny. "I would have joined Yehudah Hamaccabee's army and chased the Syrian-Greeks right out of the Land of Israel!"

"I would have refused to bow down to the Greek idols," said Bina, "just like Chanah and her seven sons."

"I would have cleaned out the *Beis Hamikdash* and watched the *Kohen Gadol* light the new menorah."

"And I would have kept Shabbos and Rosh Chodesh and taught my children Torah, even though Antiochus warned the Jews not to!"

"I wish we could have been there," sighed Benny.

"Well," chirped Chaggai HaYonah, "if you listen carefully, perhaps we can all go back, into the Land of Israel and the story of Chanukah!"

ong, long ago, over two thousand, one hundred and fifty years to be exact, the Land of Israel was part of the great Greek empire. The Syrian-Greek king Antiochus Epiphanes wanted everyone in his empire to look and act and think like the Greeks, and most of the people did. They worshiped Greek gods and ate and dressed just like Greeks. There were even some Jews who wanted to be like the Greeks. They were called Misyavnim, from the Hebrew word *Yavan* — Greece. But many other Jews insisted on keeping the Torah, just as they had always done.

Antiochus wanted *all* of the Jews to be like the Misyavnim. He decreed that the Jews in the Land of

Israel could no longer keep the *mitzvos* in the Torah. There would be no more sacrifices on the *mizbeach* — the altar in the *Beis Hamikdash*; there would be no more Shabbos; no more circumcision for Jewish boys; no more Rosh Chodesh — the new month.

Instead, his soldiers put a statue of the Greek idol Zeus into the Temple in Jerusalem and sent idols to all the cities in Israel. They ordered the Jews to sacrifice pigs and eat their meat and other forbidden foods. Many Jews ran away and hid, but many others were afraid. They did whatever the Greeks told them to do.

"I wouldn't have listened to Antiochus," said Bina.

"Me neither!" said Benny. "I would have run away to the caves or the mountains!"

Mattisyahu was an old *Kohen* from the famous priestly family of Chashmonai. He and his five righteous and brave sons lived in the town of Modiin. One day, the Greeks set up an idol right in the middle of Modiin! When one of the Misyavnim tried to sacrifice to the idol, Mattisyahu took a sword and killed the man on the spot!

"*Mi Lashem eilai!*" he cried. "Whoever is for G-d, come to me!" And they did. Thousands of Jews came to Modiin to fight the Greeks.

Mattisyahu appointed his son Yehudah commander of the Jewish army. Yehudah was called the Maccabee — the Hammer — because he pounded away at the enemy. מַכַּבִּי is also the abbreviation of *"Mi Chamocha Ba'eilim Hashem* — Who among the powerful is like You, G-d!"

Yehudah's faithful soldiers hid in caves or lay in ambush. They attacked the Greeks from the rear, or in the middle of the night, and then ran away before they could be caught.

Even though the Jewish army was smaller, weaker and poorer than the mighty Greek army, they were victorious because *Hashem* helped them in their battles. Then, to the great surprise of the Greeks, the Jews succeeded in chasing them out of Jerusalem!

"I bet Yehudah would have made me his second in command!" sighed Benny.

"I don't think so!" said a practical Bina. "You're too young. Besides, he had his four brothers — Shimon, Yochanan, Yonasan and Elazar!"

"Then maybe I could have been the sixth in command!" insisted Benny.

"Shhh . . . let's listen to Chaggai tell the story!"

When Yehudah entered the *Beis Hamikdash,* he saw a sight too terrible to describe. Everything was filthy, broken, ruined and full of Greek idols!

The Jews went to work immediately. They washed, cleaned, scrubbed, repaired and rebuilt. And they made a new menorah to replace the one the Greeks had taken away. On the 25th day of Kislev, they finished their work. Everything was in perfect order. They were finally ready to rededicate the *Beis Hamikdash* to *Hashem.*

"I know what happened then! Let me tell it!" cried Bina. "They couldn't light the menorah because there was no oil! The Greeks had broken the seals on all the jugs of oil, just to spoil them!"

"Right!" said Chaggai, and he continued . . .

In order to light the menorah, only the purest olive oil, prepared especially for this task, could be used. This oil was kept in jugs which were sealed to ensure their purity. But the Greeks had broken all the seals so that the Jews could never use them again. And now there was no pure oil to be found. The *Kohanim* searched all through the *Beis Hamikdash* while everyone waited anxiously.

Then, just as they were ready to give up, someone found one unbroken jug of oil which the Greeks had not seen. This jug was even stamped with the seal of the *Kohen Gadol* — the High Priest.

"I bet if I had been there, I would have found it!" said Benny excitedly.

"Perhaps you would have," said Chaggai with a smile.

Unfortunately, there was only enough oil in the flask to last for one day, and it would take eight days to make new oil. But the Jews did not want to postpone the *mitzvah*. And so, amidst much thanksgiving, the menorah was lit and the *Beis Hamikdash* was rededicated on the 25th day of Kislev.

"What happened the next day when the oil was finished?" asked Bina.

"Bina!" cried Benny. "You know what happened next!"

"Of course I know, but I want to hear it again anyway!"

"Nothing happened," said Chaggai. "That is to say, the oil just kept burning. On and on, right through the second and third and fourth and fifth day, all the way until the eighth day when the new supply arrived.

"And that," he added when he finished the story, "is why we celebrate the miracle of Chanukah."

"And that," said Benny, "is why we celebrate for eight days."

"And that," said Bina, "is why we say the prayers *Hallel* and *Al Hanissim* on Chanukah, because it's a time of praising and thanking *Hashem* — for all Jews, in all times, in all places!"

I would have fought if Mattisyahu or Yehudah needed me," said Bina.

"Let me tell you about two women who did fight, in their own way," said Chaggai. "In fact, two of the most famous Chanukah heroes were women — Chanah and Yehudis."

Yehudis was the daughter of Mattisyahu, the sister of Yehudah Hamaccabee. She was very beautiful and Holofernes, a Syrian-Greek general, invited her to his tent. She came, and she fed him a large portion of cheese which made him very thirsty. So she brought him wine to drink. Lots of it. He drank all the wine and fell into a deep sleep, and Yehudis promptly raised his sword and cut off his head!

She was really brave! She carried the general's head into the Syrian-Greek camp; and when the soldiers there saw it, they were so frightened that they all ran away!

hanah was brave too, but in a different way. She had seven sons. King Antiochus commanded Chanah's sons to bow down to an idol. One after another, her six older sons refused, and each was killed. When the seventh and youngest boy was called, Antiochus felt sorry for him. He wanted to give the little boy a chance to save his life without *really* bowing to the idol. So he dropped his ring on the ground and told the boy to bend down and pick it up. If he did, Antiochus would spare his life. But the little boy knew that the people who were watching could not see the small ring. They would think the boy had bowed to the idol. Therefore he refused to pick up the ring. He didn't want anyone to even *think* he had bowed. So he too was taken away and killed.

"How awful!" cried Bina.

"What happened to Chanah after her sons were killed?" asked Benny.

Chanah went up to the roof and cried out: "*Hashem!* Avraham Avinu was willing to give You his one and only son, Isaac, but his son was spared. I, however, have given You all seven of my sons for the sake of Your Torah and You accepted them all!" Then she threw herself down from the roof and returned her soul to G-d.

Bina wiped her eyes. Even Benny was sniffling.

"Chanah was a very great woman," said Chaggai. "And her sons were great too. And that's why, more than two thousand years later, we still remember and learn about them."

ummy!" said Benny. "You're getting to be a really good cook, Bina. These potato latkes are delicious."

"Aren't they? They're fried in hot, fresh oil, to remind us of the miracle of the oil in the menorah! Imma made *sufganiyot,* too."

"*Sufganiyot?* What are they?" asked Benny as he finished off another latke.

"*Sufganiyot* are jelly doughnuts, fried in oil and filled with jelly. That's what people in Israel eat on Chanukah. Here, have one!"

"Do we have anything with cheese, in honor of Yehudis?"

"Of course!" said Bina. "Big, fat, sweet cheese blintzes. Here they are. I wouldn't forget Yehudis and how she fed cheese to Holofernes."

"Chanukah can be a pretty fattening holiday," said Benny with his mouth full.

"Then don't eat so much!" laughed Bina. "Just because the Jewish people are compared to olive oil doesn't mean that you have to get fat!"

"Why are we compared to olive oil?" asked Benny as he took a sugary *sufganiyah.*

"Because olive oil doesn't mix with any other liquid; it always rises to the top. And the Jewish people weren't made to mix with the other nations; they always rise to the top too!"

"Hmm . . . I wonder what fried birdseed tastes like . . ."

"Where's your dreidel, Bina? We can play while the candles are burning."

Bina took a dreidel out of her pocket. "I bought a new one. The letters on my old dreidel were all scratched out. These are shiny and clear: Nun, Gimmel, Hey, Shin. *Nes Gadol Hayah Sham* — a big miracle took place there."

Benny took out his old dreidel. "I like the one Abba brought from Israel last year. In Eretz Yisrael the letters are different, remember? Nun, Gimmel, Hey, Pey. *Nes Gadol Hayah Po* — a big miracle took place *here!*"

They sat down on the floor and took turns spinning.

"What are you going to do with the money that Bubby and Zeidy gave us for Chanukah gelt?" asked Bina as she watched her brother's dreidel turn round.

"I haven't decided yet. What will you do with yours?"

"I think I'll buy a set of pencils with my name printed on them and I'll save the rest for a present for Imma's birthday. Oops! You won that round, Benny! I guess your Eretz Yisrael dreidel is luckier than mine!"

"Let's try again. Maybe you'll win this time."

 ell Benny, I think we've learned just about all there is to learn about Chanukah, don't you?"

"No, we haven't! Did you know that Chanukah and Purim are sort of related?"

"Um . . . let me think. . . I know why!" Bina jumped up. "Neither day is mentioned in the Torah. The miracles of Chanukah and Purim both happened long after the Jews received the Torah. They are both holidays which the Jews merited all by themselves, through their own good deeds."

"Right! How did you know that? Did you learn it in school?"

"Nope," said Bina. "I thought of it myself."

"You're pretty smart today!"

"Benny," said Bina excitedly, "Chanukah may not be mentioned in the Torah, but there are hints in the Torah! Chanukah is the story of the Chashmonaim and it begins on the 25th day of Kislev. And Chashmonah was the name of the 25th place the Jews camped at in the desert after leaving Egypt! Did you know that?"

"Yep!" said Benny proudly. "And I bet we can find even more hints than that. I'm going to ask my teacher first thing tomorrow morning!"

"Do you know what the 25th word in the Torah is? Open up to — *Bereishis* — the first book in the Torah — and start counting. It's a Chanukah surprise!"

On the last night of Chanukah, Bina put her chin in her hands and watched the flickering candles. "I love Chanukah," she whispered. "These eight little candles bring G-d's light to all the Jews. They're like stars that light up our entire world."

"That's why we put them in the window," said Benny, "so that everyone will see and know that *Hashem* protects the Jewish people. He helps the weak, and the pure, and the righteous who keep His Torah, even if they aren't as big and strong as the other nations!"

"We have a lot to be thankful for, don't we?" said Bina softly. "The Torah and all the *mitzvos;* the wonderful miracles G-d did for us in the past; the things He does for us now; and best of all, another *Beis Hamikdash* to look forward to in the future! *Chanukah Sameach,* Benny. Have a joyful Chanukah!"

"*Chanukah Sameach* to you, too, Bina."

"And *Chanukah Sameach* to you all — from me, Chaggai HaYonah!"

Before you can light your own Chanukah menorah, you have to know just what to do. So here is an outline of the most important rules. If you have any questions, be sure to ask your parents or your teacher.

RULES FOR LIGHTING THE MENORAH

1. Use a nice, clean menorah in order to fulfill the special commandment of *hiddur mitzvah* — doing the *mitzvah* in a beautiful manner.

2. The menorah should be put in a doorway opposite the *mezuzah,* or in a window where it can be seen from the street.

3. You can light with candles, but oil is even better. Olive oil is the best because that's what they used in the *Beis Hamikdash.*

4. On the first night, put one candle (or oil and wick) on the right side of the menorah. Each night, we add one new candle to the left. We always start lighting from the newest candle, from left to right.

5. The lights should all be the same height and in a straight row. The candles should be far enough apart so that you can see each one separately.

6. We use a different candle to light the menorah. This candle is called the *shammash.* After the other candles are lit, we put the *shammash* higher (or lower) or in front of the other candles, so everyone will know that it is not one of the regular Chanukah lights.

7. We do not use the light from the candles for anything. They are only to look at and to see. But we *are* allowed to use the light from the *shammash.*

8. The candles should be lit at the beginning of the night, either right before or right after *Maariv,* the evening prayer. If this is not possible, they can be lit later.

9. The first night, we say three blessings . . .
   . . . *asher kideshanu b'mitzvosav vetzivanu lehadlik ner shel Chanukah.*
   . . . *she'asah nisim la'avoseynu bayamim haheym bazeman hazeh.*
   . . .*shehecheyanu vekiyemanu vehigianu lazeman hazeh.*
   The other seven nights, we say only the first two blessings.
   Each night after the blessings, we sing *Haneiros Halalu* and *Maoz Tzur.* Many people sing certain psalms from Tehillim, too.

10. The candles must burn for at least half an hour.

11. Women don't work during the time the candles are burning, because they had a special share in the miracle.

12. On Friday evening, we light the Chanukah candles first, and the Shabbos candles afterwards. We use bigger candles or more oil so that they will burn until half an hour into the night. On Saturday nights, the candles are lit when Shabbos is over.

GLOSSARY

Beis Hamikdash — the Holy Temple in Jerusalem

Bereishis — Genesis, the first book of the Bible

Bubby (Yiddish) — grandmother

Chashmonaim — the Hasmonean family

dreidel (Yiddish) — the four-sided top used for Chanukah games

Eretz Yisrael — the Land of Israel

gelt (Yiddish) — money

grogger (Yiddish) — a noisemaker used on Purim

hallel — praise; a prayer praising G-d

Hashem — G-d

hiddur mitzvah — fulfilling a *mitzvah* in a more beautiful way

Kohen — a priest in the *Beis Hamikdash*

Kohen Gadol — the High Priest in the *Beis Hamikdash*

Maariv — the evening prayer

menorah — (a) the seven-branched candelabrum in the *Beis Hamikdash;* (b) the eight-branched Chanukah candelabrum

mezuzah — a hand-written parchment containing the prayer *Shema Yisrael,* rolled up and placed on the doorposts in Jewish homes

mitzvah, mitzvos — a commandment, commandments

mizbeach — the altar in the *Beis Hamikdash*

Rosh Chodesh — the beginning of a new month

Shabbos — the Sabbath

zeidy (Yiddish) — grandfather